COPYRIGHT

All rights reserved. No part of this publication maybe reproduced in whole or in part, or stored in a retrieval system, or transmitted in any form or means electronic mechanical, photocopying, recording, or otherwise without written permission of the publisher.

Text copyright © Sarah Dobbs

The Heartless Disconnections

2050 and The World was heartless. Meaning it had 'less' hearts that were actually natural ones, that a baby was normally born with.

In 2034 The World had become very unhappy and unhealthy. Humans were eating themselves to death, taking addictive substances or sometimes taking their own lives.

Science and technological advances were just starting to take the World's unchallenged attention and a solution was proposed.

An obesity and aesthetic miracle drug that would actually change your DNA and brain impulse signals to be healthier and be happier.

Unfortunately, side effects resulted in heart defects.

In 2044 as a result, the Government had to bring in 'The Cardiac Directive' legislation. All babies who had the defective genealogy would have their hearts removed at birth and a synthetic one inserted…………..

Dedicated to:

Angie White who brought 'The Heartless' to life with her creative, imaginative, and unique book cover.
We all need each other to bring things together.
We are all unique and creative. We all have hearts.
Thank you, Angie, from my heart.

The Heartless Disconnections

Asgre knew throughout history, the 'World' could catalogue an entire city with accounts of heartless and brutal atrocities. Saying that however there used to be some light, some heartfelt and brave deeds, some choice in the heart that you wanted to have. The 'World' (today in 2050, there is no name for where we live), has taken that away that choice. The choice of being able to be led by your natural 'heart-felt' instincts – good or bad. Cold, icy, inhuman.

People get used to everything eventually. But Asgre was old enough to remember the days when the World had a name, that where you lived had a name and that you could even name your house. Everything is a symbol now except bizarrely you were allowed to name your child (but only from a limited list). People would pre-register their children's names as soon as they knew they were pregnant because there was a quota limit on the names. So, the most popular names were quickly snapped up. The World however was heartless, literally. You could name your baby but when your baby was born you had to consent to the World replacing your baby's heart with a synthetic BFSD (Blood Flow System Device). Like I said 'heartless.

Asgre still had her human heart, although she was amongst the minority of the World population. Under regulation HRD (Heart Replacement Directive) she was allowed to keep her own heart because it was not diseased. There was no history of diabetes, stroke, obesity, heart failure or mental illness in two consecutive generations of her family.

Sure, throughout history the World had known health issues that put fear into people's hearts such as influenza epidemics in the early 2020's, but the events of 2034 were going to alter history and change humanity. No one saw it coming. No one really cared and no one asked any questions. Science was science, safe, effective, advanced etc etc and no questions asked. Trust the science. And why not? People did not trust Nature or their own environment. Life was too fast and too convenient. Science was reliable.

Asgre had grown up in the country by the sea. She respected and loved Nature. Nature was her safe place and the effect of feeling the sand beneath her feet and staring out to sea while the waves soothed her soul was the best medicine she could take. She also asked questions. Sometimes too many and it really annoyed people around her. Well, she used to ask questions out loud but now she internally asked them to herself. Too much censorship, too many questions that would not be answered anyway. She had learned to be selective and especially now she had responsibility.

Asgre was asking herself so many questions now and raising her already high blood pressure to a dangerous level. "This is no good for my baby. I must stop this agonising now," she said to herself sternly. She still did wonder how it all went so wrong and then remembered it was just an experiment 'gone wrong.' Very wrong.

This is what happened:

By 2034 the World had become very unhappy and unhealthy (It was called 'Earth' then. There were different countries, with different names but they all were suffering).

To be fair the scientists and health professionals tried to educate people and change self-destructive habits. A lot of money was spent on government incentives and education to encourage people to take more exercise and eat less 'fast' food. They were warned and warned and yet they still ate, drank, and smoked too much and moved very few body parts except fingers for texting and game playing and the eyeballs for surfing the net and social networking. And so, the shutters came down on the Welfare State, closed for business.

There was just not enough money and resources to cope with the ill health. Chaos started to unfold. We cannot have chaos, can we?

'No,' said the World.

And then the stable, reliable scientific and technological advances in medical research suggested a solution to the problem. A new obesity and aesthetic miracle drug was trialled and offered to the needy population. It worked by changing your DNA and brain impulse signals to become both healthier and happier. It sounded too good to be true and it was free. Almost the whole adult population took the drug even if they were not in need of it because it offered them future protection. A passport to living an indulgent and hedonistic life but with no consequences. Who would not want this?

Asgre did not take the drug. She was 'old fashioned' and believed in cooking 'from scratch' and exercising daily.

In other words, she just didn't feel she needed it, a kind of gut instinct and a foreboding feeling kind of repelled her at the time. Asgre was very intuitive and this time especially her intuition proved to be right. Even though she did not want to be 'right.' She had tried to tell a few friends of her bad 'feelings' but everyone thought she was being a drama queen. The truth, the connection to the drug and subsequent ill health took ten years to be acknowledged as 'causal.'

So, that is what happened. People messed their lives up, the World tried to save them but messed their lives up. Lives were a mess.

More than a mess really.

As unfortunately, side effects of the drug resulted in congenital heart defects and because the DNA was changed. This meant future generations would also inherit the defective gene and life expectancy was estimated to be no more than 20 years of age.

Some babies were not even surviving the trauma of the birth, and their hearts stopped as soon as they left the womb. This was devastating to the World and Asgre felt helpless, guilty, and remembered that time was very dark.

And so, this prompted the decision by the World to 'take no chances.'

Another solution was presented to people to resolve the problem, and the World decided this was the resolution. The only way to save humanity was to help the human race artificially. Humans were weak.

But the solution was not an 'option,' it was mandatory unless you had not taken the miracle wonder drug, 'Mana.' Ironically, the drug was no miracle cure, and because of the irreversible DNA damage man did nothing but 'wonder'…. what could they do now? Ironically, the resolution to the problem was another wonder of science.

What was proposed was the SRU (Surgical Rehabilitation Units). What happened there was kept secret and not really talked about. The Infantile Cardiac Replacement Program was set up and all the populaces knew was that all babies who were affected by the Mana drug would have a synthetic heart inserted at birth and this would ensure that they lived full and long lives. Technology was extremely advanced and though the solution was to some people 'shocking' it was the only solution.' Beggers cannot be choosers,' as Asgre's grandmother used to say.

Back to 2050. Back to 'now.'

By 2050 even though Asgre had not taken the drug the regulations now insisted on everyone having their babies heart removed.

Asgre kept thinking about being summoned to the Maternity Unit. She had no idea why they kept this old-fashioned name for the unit, out of a sick sense of nostalgia or to make the mums less frightened. It did not work as Asgre was terrified. Her birthing day was in two black screen sessions. Everybody had a personal wrist monitor that was inserted at the SRU. Coloured screens indicated the days and changed colour in 10 screen rotation as this was considered more practical than seven. In any case it was not long before her baby would have its heart ripped out.

All Asgre's friends told her she was being dramatic, and it was her hormones and her natural heart causing her all this pain and anxiety. They even suggested that she should have her heart voluntarily replaced at the same time! God, if it wasn't so real it would be funny.

What should she do? What could she do? She had been saving a much as she could for an upgraded heart and she knew that, yes, they were very reliable, and people lived much longer with the HRD's that they had ever done but it seemed wrong so wrong to have a heartless world.

Asgre was tired of thinking. Her heart was breaking but she knew that this was partly her own fault. She was one of the people who help set up the Infantile Heart Replacement program. She worked for the Ministry of Medicine. She wanted to help people. She wanted to save the World.

Her wrist monitor was flashing red and a mechanical and a soothing woman's voice was saying on repeat 'book your selection and choosing appointment.' Asgre got a black headscarf and wrapped it around her wrist and then put on her headphones. She thought to herself sadly, 'I can't ignore it once it turns black as they will just come and escort me and I will have no choice, and my maternity score will plummet.'

Everything was churning, churning in Asgre's mind.
Of course, it was only natural for mums to be nervous, but something had happened at work in the Medical Ministry yesterday and she was questioning again, and her gut instincts were screaming insider her.

Asgre wondered what life was all about.

While she was wondering she felt a tiny, somewhat uncomfortable twinge in her left side of her rounded belly. 'Ah' she thought to herself, 'I wonder if this is the Universe telling me to stop wondering as what life is about is right inside me.' If only it were that simple.

She still wondered. Still thinking.
She couldn't help but wonder and think as she looked out the window at her sister's children playing.

She had come to live with her sister when she had the shock of finding out that she was expecting a child. She had been told by numerous doctors that she could not have children after the cycling accident she had as a reckless teenager.

No teenager thinks about the future only having fun and adventure and that is how it should really be anyway. Not like it is now. Teenagers are shut indoors, confined to areas, and permitted only to cross the area when it is deemed a 'privilege' authorised by the Movement Authority. In fact, no one can leave their Locs (locations) unless a requisition has been approved. Asgre and her sister were incredibly lucky. Their family had moved to the Bay Locs in the early 2000's and it was an area of sandy beach, woods, and hills. She didn't have to use any of her well-being 'privileges or work overtime to earn requisition to leave her Locs. She was content and she was grateful.

She was lying down in the beautiful window seat of the gothic mansion, her black maternity suit starting to get too small and the heat making her feel 'sticky.' It was a red velvet window seat with red cushions edged with gold tassels. Asgre loved these cushions, they gave her a kind of comfort to twist the tassels as her mind wandered.

It was the end of the summer, and the wind was slightly more chilly than normal even though the sun shone. The Autumn was sneaking in on the breeze, Asgre could just feel it.

Asgre's sister, Silva was wealthy. She was very generous and very 'showy.' Asgre was grateful though as her baby's father was not around nor was, he ever going to be around. They told her she could not have children, so she didn't bother with any 'precautions' as they were extremely difficult to obtain. The World wanted children. The population was declining every year and fertility rates low in both men and women. Her sister had two by medical procedure, the 'terrible twins' as she called them and not affectionately. Spoilt, rude and very detached from emotion. Asgre had never seen them cry, even as babies they would just kind of whimper and sometimes just loud grunts to get attention.

She twisted the golden tassels on the cushions and just stared at Silva's children outside. Every day for the past ten screen days she watched them play and every day the same toys, the same swing and the same everything. She couldn't hear the conversation, but she did wonder if that was the same also.

They exhibited strange behaviours, occasionally they would just turn to each other and smile and stare into the distance as if something was calling them. Other times they would turn their heads to the side and sort of 'twitch' like there was a glitch in their systems. What was most unusual thought was that no animal would be alone with them and leave the room if they stroked them. Even flowers (only rich people had real flowers), seemed to turn their heads away when they passed them by. It was everything was connected in the World, yet Nature was selectively disconnecting.

No one else seemed to notice these things even though she had tried to talk to her sister.

Still fiddling with the golden tassels Asgre stopped suddenly. Something was not right with the twins; they weren't doing the same thing that they always did. The youngest seemed to be 'zigzagging' when he moved, and the eldest one just sat smiling. They both got up to leave the garden heading in the direction of the beach. Strange. Asgre got up to tell Silva but then she burst into the room as she always did like the World was on fire.

'Spying still?' Silva burst into the window seat room. 'You should be booking your 'choose and select' appointment not daydreaming like you always do.'

Silva was so bossy and never had understood Asgre and there was no way she could tell her sister what had happened at work.

This is what happened at work.

Every month the line managers like Asgre must have 'happy' consultations with their staff. Normally everything was always fine, working for the Ministry was a stable job with good prospect of getting extra 'privileges.' Last week Asgre invited Rosie in for her post-natal chat. As soon as Rosie walked through the door Asgre sensed something was wrong. Rosie sat down and stared at her feet. Then she started tapping her feet and then she got up and started pacing and then she sat back down and stared blankly across the table at Asgre.

'I am not happy. I am not happy. I am not happy.

Then Rosie's eyes went cold, and she told her story.

'I was so looking forward to having my baby. I had a great family support, and they paid for a golden heart for the little one.' (I have not named her yet; I can't find the right name from the list) …. no, that is a lie. I can't name her because I don't know how to connect with her and all I feel is pain and loss and the need to search this World until I find my daughter's heart and re-connect her to her soul.

When they first take you to the Maternity Unit, they give you a shot to make you drowsy. Everything is lovely in there and luxurious. Bedrooms facing the sea, tea and coffee facilities and all the 'baby stuff' you will need for your stay. I was quite excited and looking forward to the birth. I was being looked after.

After a few hours, a pre-op nurse came to visit to explain everything about the birthing procedure and to answer any questions. She said I would give birth as normal, unless of course there were complications and then I would have a Caesarean section and be put to sleep. She assured me that there would be plenty of pain relief drugs and not to worry at all.

She then looked at me and gently said that one thing the Maternity Unit hadn't mentioned was probably the most important thing.

The nurse explained that years ago, mothers were given the baby to hold straight after birth to encourage bonding. I was told that I could hold my baby's heart just for one second before it was taken away and the gold heart put in. This would be my bonding, and it was important. Especially important.

My friends had not told me about this and I was a bit stunned. But I trusted the medical staff and I wanted my baby to live a ong and disease-free life. I thought it was quite kind of them to let a mum hold her baby's heart.

After some consideration I decided I would wait and see how I felt when I saw my baby. The main thing was that my baby would live. I knew of lots of babies in the 2040's who didn't live past their teenage years and the thoughts of this happening to my baby was unbearable.

What I didn't know was going to be unbearable was holding my baby's heart in my hands and then letting it go like it was a piece of meat. If felt so wrong.

And they lied about the pain relief. There was no pain relief because they don't want the baby's heart damaged or put under any undue stress. I could hear them talking in hushed whispers when I asked for it. All they did was call for a doctor to perform a Caesarean without anaesthetic. Painful but not as painful as having a precious beating and beautiful heart placed in your hands for one magical minute and then snatched away. I got pain relief then. I was given a drug that was supposed to make me forget but somehow, I remember everything. I didn't straight away. When I first woke up in my luxurious Maternity suite with my perfect baby, I was happy.

It was when I returned home, and I started to have flash backs and little snippets of faces that scared me. Then eventually I remembered.

I remember everything from that day. I remember the pain of the delivery; I remember the smell of the disinfectant. I remember the messenger man dressed in scrubs standing next to what looked like a cool box with a serpent's head engraved on the side. I remember him looking at me with dead, black eyes of impatience. I remember that day, and I am not supposed to.

I remembered that the only reason they let you hold the heart was so that it would not stop beating. A baby's heart will connect only with the natural mother's heart after birth. They needed that connection to keep the heart beating.

You see Asgre, they give you a drug straight after you have held your baby's heart to make you forget the connection, to make you forget the pain and to make you drowsy so you don't see the heart being wrapped up and sent away with a special messenger who is standing right by your bed.

Rosie was talking very quickly and was clearly agitated by the memories. Asgre was becoming increasingly agitated too and she put her hand protectively on her belly. Instinct was a powerful thing and a mother's instinct and in-built protection for her baby was by far the most powerful instinct in Nature.

The World had lost touch with Nature, the World had become trans Nature, robotic and soulless. Asgre wanted Rosie to stop talking but she also wanted more information.

Asgre asked 'how can I help? How can I make you happy?

Rosie gripped Asgre's hand. 'You can't.'

She continued her story. This time Rosie spoke calmly.

'I have only come to this meeting to warn you. To plant seeds before you go for your birthing day so you might remember something. I do not know how this can help you. I just felt the need to tell you. You are kind and you are trusting and your have love in your heart.'

Then Rosie left.

After a long cry in the toilets Asgre told her bosses, and they looked concerned. They made Rosie an appointment with the hospital. She had to tell them, or it would have looked very suspicious. They would have heard everything anyway. All offices were monitored by visual and audio equipment.

Her bosses told her that sometimes the drugs they give you in a particularly difficult birth can cause antenatal psychosis and depression. They assured her that this was exceedingly rare and not to worry.

That was fine for them to say, Asgre was about to give birth any day and she now was thinking that she wanted to keep her baby and its natural heart. She had so many other questions other than why no one tells you about the 'heart-holding.' Like, where did the hearts go?

She wanted to ask Rosie the next day, but Asgre never saw Rosie again.

Back to the story:

Asgre looked calmly at her annoying sister and changed the subject quickly.

'I am not spying, just watching and I have just watched you kids head off to what looks like the beach. I thought you did not like them going out the garden without you?'

Silva rushed to the window flinging the cushions on the floor and pressing her nose against the window scouring the garden for her precious twins.

'Buzz Miko and tell him to meet me at the pier. I am sure I will find them if they have their phones with them, I just cannot see them on my tracker device now, but it is due for a service soon. You stay here in case they come back or just wandered out a little bit.'

Her face was white, and she was trying not to panic.
Asgre nodded and took her place back at the window seat and waited, fiddling with the tasselled cushions, and thinking how times have changed. She had so much freedom as a child, running wild on the beach without tags, only going home to have something to eat and then back out again. Collecting snails to put in a snail garden, eating blackberries straight from the bush, climbing trees and scrumping apples and damsons, jumping over streams and building dens. Part of Asgre was pleased the twins had escaped but this was not like them, and they never changed their routines or their minds. That is what disturbed Asgre the most. People change their minds all the time, it is what makes them human. The twins never changed their mind.

They once decided that they were going to the zoo on a day out but they zoo had been closed for some maintenance.

Nothing could persuade them to go somewhere else, not chocolate, not a new computer game or a visit to a theme park. They would not change their minds. Asgre laughed to herself as she was always changing her mind!

'BEEP, BEEP, BEEP'

Oh, shit it's turned black' Asgre stared at her monitor. Up the driveway came the car. 'Ministry of Medication' emblazoned proudly across both sides and the black light flashing.

They did not knock on the door; they didn't need to. The Ministry officers had right of entry to all Locs areas and to all residences.

'Oh, Hi Rex' muttered Asgre. She liked Rex, he worked on the floor above her office, and they often shared some green tea and a natter at lunchtime. The other guy with him she didn't know but he looked nice, he had a nurses' uniform on and had a red rose copper wrist band which glistened in the sunlight catching her attention, causing her to feel slightly dizzy for a moment. He saw her reaction and quickly tucked it up his sleeve and smiled at her. A nice smile, not a creepy smile.

Rex put his hands over the cuffs on the side of his belt but then took them off.

'We don't need these, do we?' he stared at her like he really didn't know her at all.
Asgre nodded and stood up.

'I just need to leave a buzz message for my sister to tell her I have gone to the hospital.

She has gone to look for her kids at the beach.'
Rex looked concerned. Missing kids were always a priority to the Ministry but so were 'choosing and selection appointments.'

'I am going to have to call this in,' said Rex.
'Ok, I can take Asgre to the hospital for her appointment no problem. Find those kids, we need them,' the nurse smiled

again but this time it was slightly creepy.

As they were walking to the car Asgre asked the nurse 'What's your name?' The wind started to get stronger and the sun less strong. She looked across the Bay and the waves were getting bigger, and she thought she could see a speed boat just jetting off across the horizon but in a zig zag pattern. 'Just teenagers from the city Locs letting their hair down.,' Asgre thought fondly.

She turned to speak to the nurse. He was fiddling with this red rose wrist band again, smiling that strange smile and staring out to sea. A gold mist rose from the horizon just as the speed boat disappeared from view. His smile didn't seem creepy now for some reason. The evening sun shone down on him and his wrist band warmly glistened and bathed in the mellow rays.

'I hope they aren't heading towards the Orme and Serpent's Locs.' Nobody is allowed in that area,' the nurse gently whispered.

He gestured to the car and Asgre reluctantly but quietly stepped inside.

She knew this day would come and she had to be brave.

'What is your name? I can't just call you 'nurse' it seems so clinical. I need to know. I am not allowed much but it would be nice to be allowed to know my captor's name at least.

'Only Elliot knows my name and it's staying that way,' the nurse looked directly at Asgre. 'I am not your captor. I am not here to upset you or to cause you any harm. I know this is difficult for you and now Rex is not here I think I can talk to you. I saw your reaction to my red rose wrist band. It attracts good souls, and you are a good soul. I would like to help you.'

'Are you a robot?' demanded Asgre. Everything is 'I' and you are so wooden.
'I am not a robot,' said the nurse smiling, you insult me.

'I'm sorry,' said Asgre but the past few days have been very strange, and I am not sure who I am, who anyone is and what is real. It is like the whole World is a lie, like my whole World is a lie. Sometimes I feel like going to sleep and not waking up. Fear is an immensely powerful emotion, and I am not afraid to say I am fearful for my baby's future.'

'You are lucky, you have Elliot as your Cardiac Replacement surgeon. When you meet him, he will explain your options and you can ask all your questions. I will be your nurse and between us we will look after you and your baby.'

Asgre started to cry uncontrollably, and the nurse looked very uncomfortable. He just stared out the window muttering it is only 15 minutes to the Maternity Unit from here. Try and be calm. We do not want attention drawn to ourselves. The more compliant and resigned we are the better. Minimise all suspicion and our mission will succeed. I do take it you want to save your baby's heart?'

'Of course I do. I did not realise how brain washed I had become; how synthetic ones were the only option. Recently I have watched my sisters' children, and they do not seem to be happy or normal at all. I have watched their behaviour get increasingly strange and now they have just wandered off. I just want my baby to be complete. If it dies, it dies. There is one sure thing in life and that is death. Better to live a life with heart and soul then to be soulless and without a heart.'

The nurse nodded in approval.

'We are here,' just a few extra forms for you to fill in as we had to come and get you!'

Asgre smiled and nodded back to nurse smiley. She could not wait to meet Elliot. Nurse smiley's eyes lit up whenever he mentioned his name, and this made Asgre feel safe and hopeful. She had not had any hope until now. Her mind had been in turmoil, confusion. She always needed to 'know' even if the truth was painful, it was better than deceit and lies.

There was a queue at the reception. That was very rare in 2050 for anyone to have to wait. The nurse looked slightly nervous, so she took this opportunity to ask the nurse about his red rose copper bracelet. Was it a lucky charm, was he superstitious?

Asgre always carried a small St. Chrisopher, a gift from her mum who had been superstitious. She never revealed this as any form of symbolism was prohibited in the World in 2050.

'No,' he replied. Elliot will explain.

Forms filled out and they were ushered through into the Maternity suite. The receptionist had given Asgre a very stern look and a small lecture on keeping appointments. Sometimes nothing changes even if it looks like it has!

And there he was, stood waiting at the door like he knew they were coming. He had the white coat on and the badge and everything that looked professional and clinical, but a warm golden glow emanated from him. Asgre felt safe for the first time in her life.

We don't have much time' said Elliot.

This is my story.

'I always believed in medicine and science. Until they gave out Mana without really conducting all the trial stages. I suppose they were desperate but that is no excuse. Hippocratic Oath 'do no harm.' I was forced to give people a drug I was not a 100 per cent sure of and I started to question my role as a doctor.

I left the profession and went travelling. I even considered re training as a priest my conscience was heavy. It was in Tibet where I did meet a holy man, and he told me I had to return to be a doctor. Strangely he gave me a red rose copper bracelet and told me to seek out those who had the same. He told me I was destined for the Golden Age but first I had to help the children. I had to save their hearts. I had no idea what he was talking about, but that night I could not sleep, and I saw myself here.

That's it really. I know why I am here, and I know what I must do.'

He reached into the drawer of his desk and gave Asgre a red rose bracelet.

'This will protect you to some degree,' he said. I know you believe.'

'I do believe in you,' said Asgre. How are you going to save my baby's heart?' I don't believe a bracelet is going to be enough.'
'Ok, listen carefully and don't ask questions.'

We are watched as you know. I have my nurse who came with you today and he helps me. I don't always have him on my shifts though so my ability to save the babies is very limited at the moment but even one heart is better than no hearts at all.

I will say the umbilical cord has been wrapped around the baby's neck and there has been severe deprivation of oxygen to the heart. They only want undamaged, healthy ones. They don't check as I say the patient wants some dignity in birth and I deliver from behind a curtain. The courier from the Serpent project department then just leaves empty handed with his box and it is left to me to dispose of the useless heart.

There is no need for you to go through the ceremony of holding the heart. Once the courier has left the cameras are switched off, but I will give you an injection to help you with the trauma and pain of delivery. We just must get the courier out before the baby cries. The Heartless babies never cry.

Asgre didn't have any questions, she just hugged Elliot, and her mind found some peace. Elliot said their time was up and he gave her a slip to hand into reception for her birthing date.

'oh' said Asgre. Actually, I do have one question. A colleague of mine, Rosie mentioned a box with a serpent's head on it. You just mentioned it too. What is that all about?

They want to create a new race. The serpent project is where the Ministry take the red human heart and insert them into robots and the heart turns black. They are in developmental stages but soon they will be indistinguishable from a human. But they will have only logical brains and very few emotional impulses and they will never change their minds. Only humans have the ability to change their minds. That's what makes us special.

Asgre could not speak for a moment but then she said, 'we must fight this.'

Elliot smiled and said, 'fight for your baby first and then humanity.'

The car journey back was strangely silent. The smiley nurse dropped Asgre off at the mansion and just left without a 'goodbye.' 'He is definitely a mysterious and enigmatic man,' she thought.

She wasn't looking forward to going back into the house in case the twins were still missing.

She took a deep breath and knocked on the door. (she didn't have a key or facial recognition). Miko was there now but the twins were not. Silva was there but was a complete mess.

She could hardly recognise her sister. Her hair had been torn out in clumps, she was wet through but didn't seem to care and she was sat on the floor clutching the twin's dry clothes and just wailing like a banshee. 'What has happened, Silva? Where are the twins?' Asgre hugged her sister tightly, but she didn't seem to notice.

The clothes started to glow a bit like the light Asgre had earlier seen over the horizon of the Bay by the speed boat. They turned golden and then disintegrated. Not one thread remained. The dust rose up and covered Silva in luminous particles. There was only Asgre and Miko in the room. Miko did not lift his eyes from his phone and Silva did not open her eyes ever again. Only Asgre was witness to the most strange and disturbing event she had ever imagined she would witness. Part of her thought she was going mad.

Asgre did not hate many people, but she hated Miko. He was rude, arrogant, and treated her sister like a housekeeper most of the time. Ignoring her was nothing new but ignoring his children was really disturbing her.

She rushed over to where he was sitting, grabbed his phone, and threw it on the floor.

'Where are the twins' she said.
'What twins?' he replied.

'I am in hell,' thought Asgre I need to get out of here now.
She headed to the beach as the sea calmed her nerves. Maybe she could make sense of what she thought she saw and if she was going mad. Maybe when she returned from her walk everything would be fine.

The day had been weird but hopeful. Now she was just as confused and terrified as she had been before she had met Elliot and the smiley nurse.

Miko didn't even ask her where she was going, it was like the World had stood still in a gruesome murder scene.

Asgre grabbed her bag and some snacks from the kitchen as no matter what she had to look after her unborn baby. She slowly navigated the steep steps leading down to the beach, taking her shoes off as she reached the last step. She always liked to go bare foot wherever she could to make contact with the Earth. It was called 'grounding,' and she found that it always made her feel more 'settled' and 'energised.'

The salty air was always a nostalgic welcome smell and the soft sand like comfy slippers beneath her feet. The wind had died down in the late evening and the sun had turned orange red as it was about to say 'goodnight' to what had been such a strange day.

She decided she wouldn't walk too far and just paddle a little bit at the water's edge. In the old days she used to have to watch out for small jelly fish at the water's edges, so her eyes were always looking down. She saw them just as she was turning to go back. Two small gold rings with the twin's initials and a message written in the sand that said:

'The Soul Connectors called for us.' Who the hell were the 'Soul Connectors?' Asgre felt so out of her depth. She almost felt like walking into the sea and never coming out. Rosie had certainly rocked her reality. Thank God she had met Elliot. Though he had told her more strange things he instilled in Asgre a confidence and she felt he was a kind soul. A kindred spirit. A fighter. Just what the World needed and just what she needed.

She knew she would never walk into the sea as long as she had her baby to protect. Nobody tells you how strong this maternal instinct is and what a responsibility it is. How things change, how the future mattered more than it had before.
She was going to show Elliot.

Asgre took a picture of the rings and the message as a reminder that she was not going mad and sent them, deleting after sending. She kicked sand over the message and buried the rings as deep into the sand as she could dig with her bare hands.

She knew now that there was no turning back. She had lost her family, and she could not live with Miko, he would just treat her exactly the same as he had treated her sister. The World took care of people who went mad. Asgre thought about taking her sister with her after her baby's birth, but she knew deep down that she had to go alone.

For now, I just need to play the game. The World's a stage and I just need to play my part until the final golden curtain comes down. Asgre laughed at her own terrible cliches, but she knew if you didn't laugh you would go mad.

For now, I will return and try and help Silva and try and tolerate her vile husband Miko. I am not going to tell them about the rings or the message. I know there will be an investigation, and it will be difficult not to give anything away.

In the next few days, I will give birth, and Elliot will take care of everything. The Serpent project was not going to get her baby's heart. She was going to fight for humanity and fight for her baby's heart. Asgre touched the red rose copper bracelet that Elliot had given her. It brought her comfort and strength. She knew she was not alone.

She headed up the stone path to the house and sat back down in the window seat. Nobody had been the slightest bit interested in her. There were newspaper reporters, police investigators and a representative from the Ministry of Medicine who had subdued Silva.

Miko was talking to the police. I got up from the window seat and wandered over. It looked better for me to be the concerned Aunty, and I was. My poor sister, she was destroyed, and I could not help her.

I made my statement and returned to the window seat. Chaos everywhere.

For once I was looking forward to my birthing. It felt like a release and a new life, even though I knew it was going to be hard.

I kissed my sister 'goodnight' and went to bed. I dreamt about the Golden Age. It was the best night's sleep I had had since poor Rosie told me her story.

This was my dream.
The Golden Age.

There is no money here. There is only abundance. There is no surveillance, and we are free to move (or rather float) about as we wish.

The air is clean and noisy only with laughter.
Yes, everything is golden, the mountains, the buildings, and the sea and even the people.

There is no sadness here. There is only gratitude.
Yes, your most loved and precious ones are here with you. They never really left you.

The happiness is like you have never experienced. Contentment, joy, surprise and no angst.

And the most golden gift of all. There is peace.

The Golden Age 56

...............As with all interferences in Nature the consequences are often unforeseen and with a heavy heart humans just accepted their fate.

Well, most humans. Not everyone in The World was 'heartless', and some had beautiful souls as well as brave hearts.

2050. Asgre, a heartbroken 'mother to be' meets Elliot, her baby's cardiac surgeon at her 'choosing and selection' appointment. He gives her a red rose and the fight for The Golden Age begins.

Printed in Great Britain
by Amazon